Tom and Jill

by Pauline Cartwright
illustrated by Bettina Guthridge

Harcourt
SCHOOL PUBLISHERS

Printed in China

ISBN 10: 0-15-350341-6
ISBN 13: 978-0-15-350341-2

Ordering Options
ISBN 10: 0-15-350331-9 (Grade 1 Below-Level Collection)
ISBN 13: 978-0-15-350331-3 (Grade 1 Below-Level Collection)
ISBN 10: 0-15-357392-9 (package of 5)
ISBN 13: 978-0-15-357392-7 (package of 5)

5 6 7 8 9 10   468   15 14 13 12 11 10 09

Can Tom find his hat?

There is too much here.

Come in here, Jill.

Help me.

Look in here, Tom.

You have your hat on.

Thank you, Jill.